IT IS TIME TO GO ON A HUNT

Story told and illustrated by
Tiffany A. K. Jere

First Published 2022
Book Publishing Support by
Divine Flow Publishing Ltd, UK

ISBN: 9798363113444

I dedicate this book to my parents because they helped me publish my book. I hope that this book will inspire many other children.

The book belongs to...

....◆

....◆

....◆

....◆

FORWARD:

Tiffany is a gifted and prolific story teller who has creativity in abundance. Her stories showcase her imagination and captivate the reader; I find myself wanting to read more! Not only can she entertain the reader with her tales, but her illustrations are equally as captivating. Through word and picture, Tiffany will transport you to another world with this book ~ enjoy your journey back in time and the quest to find a deer!

Mr. Adrian Bassett

Headteacher

It Is Time To Go On A Hunt...

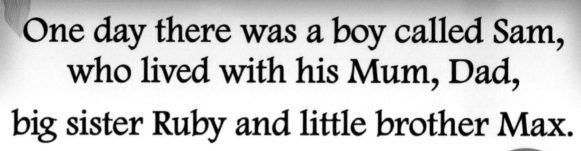

One day there was a boy called Sam,
who lived with his Mum, Dad,
big sister Ruby and little brother Max.

1

"Mum, I'm really hungry!" mumbled Sam.

"Okay that means we will need to go hunting," answered Mum as she was walking to wake up the rest of the family.

"Mum what's for breakfast?"
asked Ruby as she tiptoed to try
and scare Sam.

"I don't know what's for breakfast?"
answered Mum.

"I know just the thing!" Shouted Dad...

"Deer!"

"Off course!" Shouted Ruby excitedly.

So the whole family went out into the deep, dark forest.

So as the family went deeper into the forest, dad heard a…

…DEER!

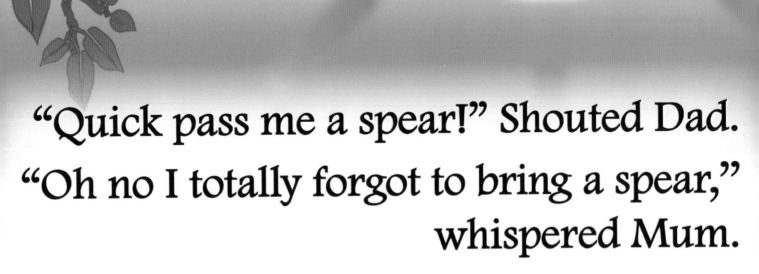

"Quick pass me a spear!" Shouted Dad.

"Oh no I totally forgot to bring a spear," whispered Mum.

"It's okay," answered Max.

"I know just the thing!"
Whispered Ruby
"What?" asked Mum.

"Max, can you please get me a stone, Sam can you please get me a large branch and Mum can you please get me a long rope or a vine?" asked Ruby.

11

"Okay,"
Mum whispered.

"Okay, so now we have the spear,
lets go and get our deer," whispered Ruby.

"5,   4,   3,   2,   1, Goooo !

Shouted Ruby as the spear flew into the air
and caught the deer.

So as the family went out of the deep, dark forest it started to rain.
"Oh no, it's raining!" Shouted Mum.
"I know let's use this large leaf," answered Ruby.

So the whole family
went back home
and ate their deer.

The

End!

ABOUT THE AUTHOR:

Tiffany Anashe Krystal Jere is an amazingly intelligent nine-year-old young writer, who has an innate ability to create stories that are not just intriguing, but also captivating.

She is determined, focused, driven and disciplined young girl.

Her favourite subjects in school are science, maths and English.

A Formula One fan who enjoys watching Wreck it Ralph, Lego Masters, Super Book, MasterChef Australia and Sonic the Hedgehog. Her favourite toys are the Trrrumpet squad, Bunny Bunny & the Bunny family.

She loves going to church every Sunday with her family.

More books coming soon...

Printed in Great Britain
by Amazon

20311602R00016